It was cold and grey outside. Jolly Tall, the giraffe, had been gazing out of the window for days.

'What are you waiting for?' asked Rabbit.

'I'm waiting for it to snow,' said Jolly. 'It is winter, isn't it?'

'It doesn't *always* snow in winter,' said Rabbit.

'In fact it hardly ever does,' said Duck gloomily.

'I know where there's some snow,' said Little Bear. 'It must be left over from last winter. I'll get it for you.'

Without waiting to explain, Little Bear rushed out of the room.

In a moment he was back again carrying a large glass bubble. Inside the bubble they could see a little house and a tree covered in a layer of tiny white snowflakes.

'Is that all snow does?' asked Jolly, staring into the bubble. 'Does it just lie around making things whiter than usual?'

'Of course not,' said Little Bear. 'That wouldn't be any fun. You can make it into balls and throw it.'

'Or slide on it,' said Zebra.

'And jump into heaps of it,' said Rabbit, 'and make footprints.'

'You can build with it too,' said Duck.

'Goodness,' said Jolly. 'There doesn't look enough of it for that.'

JANE HISSEY
Jolly Snow

Mini Treasures
RED FOX

Holding the glass bubble tightly, Little Bear jumped up and down. A flurry of snowflakes leaped from the tiny house and tree and rushed around inside the glass. 'Look at it now!' he squeaked.

'There's still not enough to make a snowball,' said Jolly.

'And anyway, you can't get it out,' said Duck.

'Wait a minute,' said Zebra. 'I know where there's lots of snow.'

She led the way to the kitchen, where Bramwell Brown was busy making some special biscuits. To stop the biscuit dough sticking to the rolling pin, he was shaking flour from a flour shaker.

'Whoopee!' cried Zebra, dashing under the falling flour. 'I'm in a snowstorm.'

In no time at all, her black stripes had almost disappeared.

Rabbit tried to gather up a pawful of the flour. 'It's not very good for snowballs,' he said. 'It doesn't stick together.'

'But it's perfect for DOUGHBALLS,' cried Little Bear, rolling up a piece of dough and throwing it at Rabbit. The doughball stuck to Rabbit's bottom and looked like an extra tail.

'This flour-snow doesn't come off,' said Zebra, jumping up and down trying to shake herself clean.

'I think you are going to need a bath,' said Bramwell.

He filled a dish with soapy water and the snowy Zebra climbed in. She began to splash about, sending bubbles flying everywhere. 'It's still not coming off,' she grumbled. 'It just gets stickier and stickier.'

'Flour and water make a sort of glue,' said Duck. 'You'll probably have to stay white for ever.'

'No you won't,' said Bramwell kindly. 'We'll get you clean.'

All the scrubbing and splashing made even more bubbles.

'Snow-bubbles!' cried Little Bear, jumping about, popping them with his paws. 'Hurry up, Zebra, we want to use your bath as a snow-machine.'

After lots of rubbing and scrubbing,
Zebra's stripes at last reappeared.
The others wrapped her in a warm
towel and looked
into the bath.

'What have you done with all the bubbles?' asked Little Bear.

'Bubbles never last,' said Duck, 'and anyway, they would have made very sloppy snow. Why don't we go and see if Old Bear has any ideas?'

Old Bear was in the dining room, cutting out paper decorations. He'd made paper stars, paper bells and paper lanterns. He'd even made paper snowflakes.

'You can't really play with these,' said Little Bear, trying to slide on a snowflake.

'No you can't,' said Old Bear, rescuing his decoration. 'They're only meant for looking at.'

'We want some snow for Jolly,' said Rabbit. 'Snow you *can* play with.'

What about these?' said Old Bear,
scattering a blizzard of paper pieces
in the air.

'Lovely,' said Rabbit.

'And nice and slippery too,' said Little
Bear, taking a run at a heap of them and
skidding along on his bottom.

'What we need is a sledge,' said Rabbit,
'or Little Bear will wear out his trousers.'
He fetched a cardboard box and
Bramwell cut away the sides.
Duck tied a string to the
front and they pulled
it along to test it.

'Now, if we had a slope,' said Rabbit, 'we could whizz down it in the sledge.'

'I don't think I could,' said Jolly. 'I wouldn't fit in it.'

'Never mind,' said Bramwell. 'You can help with the slope.' Bramwell Brown disappeared into the bedroom and came back pulling a large white sheet. He gave a corner to Jolly. 'Now,' said Bramwell, 'when the others climb on, lift up your end.'

Rabbit and Little Bear pushed the sledge onto the sheet and climbed in.

As soon as they were ready, Little Bear called out to Jolly: 'One, two, three, GO!'

J olly and Bramwell lifted their end of the sheet. Nothing happened.

'Wobble it a bit,' called Rabbit. 'We seem to be stuck.' Jolly and Bramwell shook the sheet as hard as they could and suddenly the toys found themselves sliding very fast to the other end.

'Look out,' cried Little Bear, as the sledge whizzed off the sheet, across the room and crashed into the wall on the other side.

'I think we need a softer landing,' said Rabbit, fluffing up his flattened fur and helping Little Bear to his feet. He piled up a heap of cushions against the wall and then all three toys bravely climbed back onto the sheet.

'Ready, steady, go!' they called to Jolly.

Up went the sheet.
Down went the toys –
straight into the heap of cushions.
As they landed clouds of feathers
puffed out of a little hole in
one of the cushions and
filled the room.

'Look – it's feather-snow,' cried Little Bear, making the hole bigger with his paw and jumping on the cushion to make more feathers escape. Very soon all the toys were jumping in the feathers.

'Is this like snow?' asked Jolly.

'It's better,' said Little Bear. 'It doesn't melt and it doesn't make you cold.'

'Let's put some round the windows,' suggested Rabbit. 'Then it will look as if real snow has settled there.'

He climbed up to the windowsill and began to pile feathers in each corner. When he reached the third window pane he stopped and looked, then looked again.

'Somebody has already done this one,' he called to the others. The window did have a white covering around the edges... but it was on the *outside*.

'It isn't feathers,' cried Little Bear excitedly. 'It's real snow!'

All the toys crowded onto the sill and stared out of the window in amazement.

'Now we can play outside,' said Zebra.

'Well, actually – it looks a bit deep for me,' said Little Bear.

'And a bit cold for me,' said Old Bear.

At that moment, Bramwell Brown came into the room carrying a huge plateful of his special snowflake biscuits.

'I think what you need is some of *my* snow,' he said.

Jolly Tall thought about the flour-snow and the feather-snow, the bubble-snow and the paper-snow. Then he looked at the real snow floating down outside.

'I really like all kinds of snow,' he announced. 'But,' he added, munching a snowflake biscuit, 'Bramwell's snow is probably the snow I like best!'

For Ralph

This edition first published in 1996

1 3 5 7 9 10 8 6 4 2

© Jane Hissey 1991

Jane Hissey has asserted her right under
the Copyright, Designs and Patents Act, 1988,
to be identified as the author and illustrator of this work

First published in the United Kingdom 1991 by
Hutchinson Children's Books
First published in Mini Treasures edition 1996
by Red Fox
Random House, 20 Vauxhall Bridge Road, London SW1V 2SA

Random House Australia (Pty) Limited
20 Alfred Street, Milsons Point, Sydney
New South Wales 2061, Australia

Random House New Zealand Limited
18 Poland Road, Glenfield
Auckland 10, New Zealand

Random House South Africa (Pty) Limited
PO Box 337, Berglevi, South Africa

Random House UK Limited Reg. No. 954009

A CIP catalogue record for this book
is available from the British Library

ISBN 0 09 972511 8

Printed in Singapore